Bedtime Storytime

Bath • New York • Singapore • Hong Kong • Cologne • Delhi
Melbourne • Amsterdam • Johannesburg • Shenzhen

This edition published by Parragon in 2013
Parragon
Chartist House
15–17 Trim Street
Bath BA1 1HA, UK
www.parragon.com

Written by David Bedford, Hettie Bingham, Moira Butterfield,
Caroline Pitcher, Jillian Harker, Katherine Sully, Peter Bently and Annie Baker.
Retellings by Kathryn Jewitt, Hettie Bingham, Ronne Randall,
Sarah Delmege and Gaby Goldsack.
Illustrated by Henry St Leger, Dubravka Kolanovic, Jacqueline East, Gavin Scott, Simon Mendez,
Jenny Jones, Kristina Stephenson, Gill McLean, Janet Samuel, Gail Yerrill, Polona Lovsin.
Edited by Robyn Newton
Cover illustrated by Laura Rigo
Cover design by Kathryn Davies
Production by Richard Wheeler

Every effort has been made to acknowledge the contributors to this book.
If we have made any errors, we will be pleased to rectify them in future editions.

ISBN 978-1-4723-2336-1

Printed in China

Bedtime Storytime

CONTENTS

Jack and the Beanstalk

Once, there was a boy named Jack who lived with his mother. They were very poor and had to sell their cow to get money for food.

As he was taking the cow to market, Jack met an old man.

"You won't get much money for such an old cow," he told Jack, "but I can give you something better than money for her – magic beans!"

He held out his hand and showed Jack five speckled beans. **Magic beans!** thought Jack. **They sound exciting!** He gave the old man the cow and took the beans, thanking the man politely. Then he went home to his mother.

Jack's mother was extremely cross.

"Silly boy!" she shouted. "Thanks to you, we have no cow and no money!"

She threw the beans out of the window and sent Jack straight to bed.

The next morning, Jack was astonished when he looked out of the window. A giant beanstalk had sprung up while he was sleeping, and it stretched up to the sky.

Jack ran outside and began to climb the beanstalk.

Up and up he went, higher and higher, till he reached the top.

There he found a road, which led to a big house.

Jack's tummy was rumbling with hunger, so he knocked on the large wooden door.

A giant woman answered. She looked kind and Jack asked if she would give him some breakfast.

"You will BE breakfast if my husband finds you!" she told Jack.
"He's much bigger than me, and he eats children!"
But Jack begged and pleaded, and at last the woman let him in.
She gave him some bread and milk and hid him in a cupboard.

Soon Jack heard loud footsteps and felt the cupboard shake. The giant man was coming! Jack heard him roar,

"Fee-fi-fo-fum,
I smell the blood
of an Englishman!"

"Don't be so silly," the giant's wife said. "You smell the sausages I've cooked for your breakfast! Now sit down and eat."

After wolfing down three plates of sausages, the giant asked his wife to bring him his gold. She brought two big sacks filled with gold coins, which the giant began to count. But he was sleepy after his big breakfast and soon began to snore.

Jack crept out of the cupboard and grabbed one of the sacks. Then he rushed out of the house, along the road and straight down the beanstalk.

Jack's mother was overjoyed to see him, and she was even happier when she saw the gold.

They lived well while the money lasted, but after a year it had all been spent. Once again, Jack and his mother had nothing to eat.

"Don't worry, Mother," said Jack. "I'll just go back up the beanstalk to the giant's house."

And so he did. Just as before, Jack knocked on the door and begged the giant's wife for something to eat.

"Go away," she told him. "The last time you were here, a sack of gold disappeared. My husband was really cross!"

But once again, Jack begged and pleaded, and at last she let him in. She gave him some bread and milk and hid him in the cupboard.

Soon the giant stomped in, bellowing,

"Fee-fi-fo-fum,

I smell the blood of an Englishman!"

"Nonsense," said the giant's wife. "You smell the soup I've cooked for your lunch."

Peeping through a crack in the cupboard door, Jack saw the giant slurp down a big barrelful of soup, and heard him tell his wife, **"Bring me my hen!"**

She put a fat red hen on the table, and the giant shouted,

"Lay!"

To Jack's amazement, the hen laid a golden egg!

Jack waited until the giant was asleep.

Zzzzzzzz!

Then he jumped out and snatched the hen.
Fast as lightning, he dashed out of the house,

along the road...

and

down

the

beanstalk.

17

Jack and his mother lived very well on the money
they made from the hen's golden eggs. But Jack
wanted to climb the beanstalk one last time.

He knew the giant's wife would not let him in
again, so when she wasn't looking, he
sneaked into the house and crawled
into the cupboard. Before long, the giant
came crashing in.

"Fee-fi-fo-fum, I smell the
blood of an Englishman!"
he thundered.

"You smell the steaks I've cooked for your dinner," his wife said. And she put a platter of thick, juicy steaks in front of him.

After gobbling up the steaks, the giant took out a golden harp and said, **"Sing!"** The harp played a gentle lullaby, and soon the giant was fast asleep.

Zzzzzzzz!

Jack sprang out, took the harp and began to run. But the harp cried, **"Master! Master!"**

... and the giant woke up.
With a roar, he leapt up
and ran after Jack.

Holding the harp tightly, Jack ran for his life. As he scrambled down the beanstalk, he yelled, **"Mother! Mother! Bring the axe!"**

Jack took the axe and started to chop down the beanstalk. The giant quickly climbed back up to the top before it snapped in two. That was the last time Jack saw him. With the hen and the harp, Jack and his mother were able to live happily ever after – and they were never hungry again.

The Snow Queen

Once upon a time, there was a wicked elf who made a magic mirror that showed everything in a bad light. When the mirror broke with a **crack!** hundreds of glass shards went flying out around the world.

Kai and Gerda were a little boy and girl who had grown up with each other and were like brother and sister.

One day, when they were playing outside, a shard of the broken mirror lodged in Kai's eye. Kai became very cold and unfriendly, and poor Gerda had no idea what had happened to him.

"Come and play with me, Kai," begged Gerda. She hoped that Kai would come to his senses and be friendly again. But Kai was **bitterly cold** to her, and to all around him.

"I don't want to play with you any more. Leave me alone," he said.

Kai liked the cold and the ice. Snowflakes became his favourite thing of all. He spent all day looking at snowflakes and the pretty shapes they made. Before long, the Snow Queen herself came to notice Kai, and one day she came to see him.

"I can take you to a place where it is always cold and snowy," she told Kai. And so Kai went away with her.

Nobody knew where Kai had gone, and most people thought that he must be dead.

But Gerda felt in her heart that he was still alive. She never lost faith in her old friend and vowed to find him.

Gerda set off to look for Kai wearing new red shoes. After a while she came to a river. "River, have you seen my friend Kai?" she asked. But the river would not reply. So Gerda removed her lovely red shoes, and offered them to the river.

"I will give you these new red shoes if you will help me find my friend," she told the river, and threw the shoes into the water with a splash!

The river replied:

"In my murky waters deep, many secrets do I keep.
But no boy rested his head upon my muddy river bed."

Gerda was relieved to find out that Kai had not drowned, and set off again. She walked for many miles until she came to a beautiful garden where she stopped to rest.

Gerda lay down amongst the fragrant flowers, and fell asleep. She dreamed of flowers pushing up through the soil.

When she woke up, she thought she could hear the flowers whispering to her. She listened carefully and, sure enough, a beautiful rose spoke to her:

"Beneath the ground where roots run deep, I cannot see your friend asleep."

Gerda was happy because she knew this meant that Kai wasn't dead. She set off once more to look for her dear friend.

While Gerda was walking through a forest, she met a reindeer.

"Reindeer, have you seen my friend Kai?" she asked him.

"Is he the boy who likes snowflakes?" replied the reindeer.

"Yes, they are his favourite thing," said Gerda.

The kind reindeer told Gerda that he had seen Kai in the grounds of the Snow Queen's palace. "Climb onto my back, and I'll take you there," he said. Gerda thought her heart would burst with happiness. She felt sure that she would soon find Kai and take him home. But when she and the reindeer reached the Snow Queen's land, they found that it was guarded by snowflakes.

"How will we ever get past these snowflakes?" thought Gerda. But as she walked through them, they were melted by the warmth of her heart.

Gerda and the reindeer walked through the icy land searching everywhere for Kai.

"There he is!" said Gerda, suddenly, seeing her old friend sitting in the middle of a frozen lake. She rushed over to greet him, but when she flung her arms around him, she was heartbroken to realize that Kai did not remember who she was.

"Who are you?" said Kai. "Leave me alone." But Gerda would not let go of him. She cried so hard that Kai's icy heart began to melt. Kai started crying as well, and his own tears washed the shard of broken mirror from his eye.

"Gerda, is it really you?" asked Kai.

"Yes. I've come to take you home," said Gerda.

But Kai noticed the Snow Queen riding towards them.

"We must leave this place quickly," warned Kai. "The Snow Queen will freeze our hearts and make us stay here." So Kai and Gerda climbed onto the reindeer's back and rode away from the icy land. They were never parted again and lived happily ever after.

The Velveteen Rabbit

Once upon a time, there was a Velveteen Rabbit made from soft fur, with ears lined with pink satin. When he was given to the Boy on Christmas morning, he was the best present. At first, the Boy thought the Velveteen Rabbit was wonderful, but then he put him away in the cupboard.

"What is real?" the Velveteen Rabbit asked the toys in the cupboard one day.

"It's what you become when a child really loves you," explained a hobbyhorse. "I was made real a long time ago by the Boy's uncle. It can take a very long time. By the time you are real some of your fur has dropped out. But it doesn't matter, because once you are real you can't be ugly."

One night, when Nanny was putting the Boy to bed she couldn't find his favourite toy. So she grabbed the Velveteen Rabbit by his ear.

"Here, take your old bunny!" she said. And from that night on, the Velveteen Rabbit slept with the Boy.

At first it was a bit uncomfortable. The Boy would hug him so tightly that the Velveteen Rabbit could hardly breathe. But soon he grew to love sleeping with the Boy. And when the Boy went to sleep, the Rabbit would snuggle down and dream about becoming real.

The Velveteen Rabbit went wherever the Boy went. He had rides in the wheelbarrow, and picnics on the grass. He was so happy that he didn't notice that his fur was getting shabby.

One day, the Boy left the Rabbit on the lawn. At bedtime, Nanny came to fetch the Rabbit because the Boy couldn't go to sleep without him.

"Imagine all that fuss about a toy," said Nanny.

"He isn't a toy. He's real!" cried the Boy.

When the Rabbit heard these words he was filled with joy! He was real! The Boy himself had said so.

Late one afternoon, the Boy left the Rabbit in the woods while he went to pick some flowers. Suddenly, two strange creatures appeared. They looked like the Velveteen Rabbit, but they were wild rabbits.

"Why don't you come and play with us?" one of them asked.

"I don't want to," said the Velveteen Rabbit. He didn't want to tell them that he couldn't move. But all the time he was longing to dance like them.

One of the wild rabbits danced so close to the Velveteen Rabbit that it brushed against his ear. Then it wrinkled up its nose and jumped backward.

"He doesn't smell right," the wild rabbit cried. "He isn't a rabbit at all! He isn't real!"

"I am real," said the Velveteen Rabbit. "The Boy said so." Just then, the Boy ran past and the wild rabbits disappeared.

"Come back and play!" called the Velveteen Rabbit. But there was no answer. Finally, the Boy took him home.

A few days later, the Boy fell sick. Nanny and a doctor fussed around his bed. No one took any notice of the Velveteen Rabbit snuggled beneath the blankets.

Then, little by little, the Boy got better. The Rabbit listened to Nanny and the doctor talk. They were going to take the Boy to the seashore.

"Hurrah!" thought the Rabbit, who couldn't wait to go too.

But the Velveteen Rabbit was put into a sack and carried to the bottom of the garden, ready to be put on the bonfire.

That night, the Boy slept with a new toy. Meanwhile, at the bottom of the garden, the Velveteen Rabbit was feeling lonely and cold.

He wiggled until his head poked out of the sack and looked around. He remembered all the fun he had with the Boy. He thought about the wise horse. He wondered what use it was being loved and becoming real if he ended up alone.

A real tear trickled down his velvet cheek onto the ground.

Then a strange thing happened. A tiny flower sprouted out of the ground. The petals opened, and out flew a tiny fairy.

"Little Rabbit," she said, "I am the Nursery Fairy. When toys are old and worn and children don't need them any more, I take them away and make them real."

"Wasn't I real before?" asked the Rabbit.

"You were **real** to the Boy," the Fairy said, "But now you shall be **real** to everyone."

The Fairy caught hold of the Velveteen Rabbit and flew with him into the woods where the wild rabbits were playing.

"I've brought you a new playmate," said the Fairy. And she put the Velveteen Rabbit down on the grass.

The little rabbit didn't know what to do. Then something tickled his face, and before he knew what he was doing, he lifted his leg to scratch his nose. He could move! The little rabbit jumped into the air with joy. He was real at last.

The Stubborn Prince

Once there was a stubborn prince who would **never** do as he was told. His parents despaired of him for, one day, this stubborn boy would be king.

One windy day, a new governess arrived to teach the young prince. She arrived so suddenly it was as if the wind had blown her there. The governess looked ordinary, but there was more to her than met the eye. Lessons began right away, but the prince just folded his arms and pursed his lips.

The governess wasn't worried, "I know how to deal with stubborn boys," she thought. There was a shimmer of magical lights and a huge gust of wind blew in, lifted the prince up into the air and left him hovering beneath the ceiling. At first the prince was scared, but then he began to enjoy himself.

"Ha, ha! This is fun!" he laughed. "Do it again!" he called, as the chair began to sink down.

"Not until you've done your work," replied the governess. So the prince started to work, and every time he got something right, up he'd fly again. He soon found out that joining in was fun, and he was never stubborn again.

Wish Upon a Star

If there was one thing that James wanted more than anything else, it was a new friend. He had just moved to a new area and, although he liked his new house, he **missed** his old friends.

"You'll make some new friends soon enough," his mother told him. But for now, James only had his cat, Pumpkin, for company.

James was building a den in the garden. He had found the perfect spot for it and had made some walls from tree branches. It was fun, but James thought it would be even better fun if he had a **friend** to help him.

One night when the sky was clear, James noticed the most beautiful star shining **brightly** in the sky. James thought that it might be a lucky star, so he made a wish.

"Oh, beautiful star, I wish I could make a new friend," he called up into the night.

The next day, James went out to play in his garden. He was busy working on his new den when he heard a strange noise – thwack! James looked around, but couldn't see what was making the strange sound.

Thwack! There it was again. Then, James felt Pumpkin rubbing his furry body against his leg and he bent down to give him a stroke. Pumpkin meowed loudly and ran off.

"Hey, Pumpkin!" called James. "Where are you off to?" He followed his cat, who jumped up onto the garden wall and began to meow even more loudly. He reached up to lift Pumpkin down again, and it was then that he found out where the strange sound had been coming from. Thwack!

As James peeped into the next-door garden, he noticed a boy batting a ball against the wall.

"Hello," said James. "What are you playing?"

"I'm playing tennis, but it's not much fun on my own," replied the boy.

The boy, who was called Ben, asked James if he'd like to play. James was so happy – his wish had come true! They played ball all morning and then, after lunch, they set to work finishing off James's den.

That night, James looked up at the night sky. "Thank you, star," James whispered into the night... "wherever you are!"

Thumbelina

There was once an old woman who wanted a daughter more than anything else in the world.

She went to see a witch who gave her a seed to plant. The seed grew into a beautiful flower and when the flower opened with a **pop!** a tiny little girl was sitting in the middle. The girl was no bigger than the woman's thumb, so she called her Thumbelina and loved her like a daughter. The woman gave Thumbelina a walnut shell to sleep in and made sure she had everything she wanted. Thumbelina was very happy living with her mother.

One night, an old toad-woman passed by an open window. **Hop, hoppity, hop!** She saw Thumbelina as she lay asleep in her walnut shell.

"What a tiny girl," she thought to herself. "She would make a lovely bride for my son." And the toad-woman carried Thumbelina away.

Poor Thumbelina was horrified when she woke up and saw a big warty face staring at her.

"Who are you?" she gasped.

"I am Toad, and you will be my wife," said the ugly creature. And he hopped off, leaving Thumbelina stranded on a lily pad,

while he and his mother set to
work preparing the wedding.

Thumbelina could think
of nothing worse than
being married to a toad.
She wept bitter tears,
which fell into the river
with a **splash!**

Some fish swam up to
the surface, thinking the
tear drops were insects that
they could eat. When they saw
the tiny girl crying her heart out,
the fish took pity on her.

"**Sniff!** If I can't escape from here, I'll have to marry a toad,"
sobbed Thumbelina. The helpful fish nibbled through the stem
of the lily pad, and Thumbelina floated away down the river.

The lily pad landed on a riverbank near a corn field, and
Thumbelina clambered off. She felt all alone in the world and began
to weep again. A field-mouse scuttled past and stopped to see what
was the matter.

"I am far from home," sobbed Thumbelina. "I have nobody to
care for me."

The field-mouse felt very sorry for Thumbelina. He could not
leave such a pretty creature crying and alone.

"Come and live with me, I'll look after you," he offered.

So Thumbelina lived underground where she was safe and warm. The field-mouse was very kind to her and they spent many happy days together.

The field-mouse's best friend was a mole, and he grew so fond of Thumbelina that he wanted to marry her. But the thought of living underground for the rest of her life made Thumbelina sad. She missed the open air and sunshine.

One day, as Thumbelina was walking through an underground passage, she saw a swallow. There seemed to be no life in the poor creature and, thinking he had died from cold, she wrapped him up.

But the bird wasn't dead. When he had warmed up he began to stir with a flitter, flutter! The swallow was very grateful to Thumbelina and wanted to help her.

"Come away with me," said the swallow. "We can fly off to a warmer land."

Thumbelina climbed onto the swallow's back, and together they flew over the bleak winter landscape until they noticed that the air was getting warmer and the land was becoming greener.

The swallow swooped down into a meadow full of flowers. Thumbelina thought it was the most beautiful place she had ever seen. The ground was thick with colourful blooms and the air was full of birds singing.

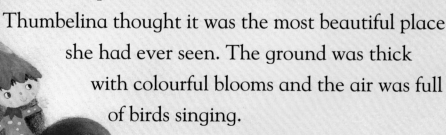

The sun shone all day long and Thumbelina felt warm and happy.

"I would like to stay here," she said. So the swallow landed, and Thumbelina jumped down from his back.

Thumbelina climbed into a lovely pink flower and breathed in its heady scent. As she looked around the meadow, she noticed that each of the flowers had a tiny sprite living in it. They were just like Thumbelina, and she felt as if she were home at last.

The king of the flower sprites flew to Thumbelina and welcomed her. When he saw Thumbelina's happy face, he fell in love and asked her to marry him. Thumbelina agreed, and they had a beautiful wedding, filled with flowers and sunshine.

Thumbelina became the queen of the flower sprites, and lived happily ever after.

I Love My Grandma

Little Hedgehog and Grandma Hedgehog loved to play hide-and-seek together. One day, when Grandma went to find Little Hedgehog...

Little Hedgehog hid! He put his paws over his mouth so that Grandma couldn't hear him giggling.

"Where, oh where can Little Hedgehog be?" said Grandma. "I want to make a tasty picnic, and I need help."

Little Hedgehog giggled again.

"Oh, well," said Grandma. "I shall have to make the picnic myself."

Little Hedgehog followed closely behind Grandma.

"I wish Little Hedgehog were here
to help me pick juicy blackberries,"
said Grandma.
When she wasn't looking, Little
Hedgehog picked the **biggest
blackberries** he could reach...
and put them into Grandma's basket!
"What a lot of berries!"
said Grandma, surprised.
"I already have enough for baking."
Little Hedgehog scampered
into Grandma's kitchen
to find the best place to hide.

Little Hedgehog crouched down low so that Grandma couldn't see him.

"If only Little Hedgehog were here to help me!" said Grandma.

Little Hedgehog giggled again.

Then he licked his lips as Grandma Hedgehog poured sweet, scrumptious honey into her mixing bowl.

"Honey is my treat for Little Hedgehog," said Grandma.

Little Hedgehog crept out from his hiding place...

He tried not to make a sound as he tasted
the honey for himself, but it was too tasty!

"Yum!"

whispered Little Hedgehog.
Then he hurried back to his hiding place. Suddenly…

"Aha!" said Grandma.
"Someone has been tasting my honey!
And they have left sticky footprints!"

"Oh, no!" Little Hedgehog didn't want to be found. Not yet!

Grandma followed the teeny, tiny, sticky **footprints** across the kitchen.

"Someone has been playing hide-and-seek with me!" she said, smiling. Then...

"I've found you, Little Hedgehog!"
said Grandma.

But Little Hedgehog wasn't behind the rocking chair. There were only more sticky footprints...

45

Grandma followed the sticky footprints out of the kitchen and into the garden. The sticky footprints went round and round and stopped by the flowerpots.

"I've found you this time, Little Hedgehog!" said Grandma. But Little Hedgehog wasn't behind the flowerpots! He was... inside one!

"**Surprise!**" said Little Hedgehog, giggling as he gave Grandma a big hug.

"Well done, Little Hedgehog," said his grandma. "You are the best at hide-and-seek. And I hope you are hungry, because our picnic is ready!"

"I am hungry!" said Little Hedgehog. But when he looked around the garden, he couldn't see a picnic anywhere. "Where is it?" he asked. Grandma giggled.

"You have to find it!" she said.

Little Hedgehog searched around the garden and soon found...

honey cookies…

and fruit salad.

Then Grandma brought out a giant blackberry and honey cake.

"Yum!" said Little Hedgehog. It was the best he had ever tasted.

"I love Grandma's picnics!"
Little Hedgehog shouted happily. "And...

"I love my grandma!"

Muddypaws

It was a special day for Ben. He had a new puppy!

"I'll teach you all the things I know," said Ben. "But first I need to choose a name for you. I'll need to think hard about it. It has to be just perfect."

"I don't really mind what name you choose, as long as
you give me lots of cuddles," thought the new puppy.

Ben looked around his bedroom to see if he could find an idea for the perfect puppy name.

"I'll look in my storybook," he said, but none of
the names in the book were right for his new puppy.

"I think I'll leave you to hunt for names," thought the new puppy. "I'd rather look behind that flowerpot."

The little puppy crept over...

He sniffed...

... and then
he climbed.

He didn't mean to
knock the flowerpot over,
but...

Oops!

That's just what he did.

He made muddy pawprints everywhere.

"Let's go to the park. I might be able to think of a good name there," said Ben.

"I'd rather look behind that tree," thought the little puppy.

So he ran...

... and he ran.

He didn't mean to
jump in the mud, but...

That's just what he did.

squelch!

He made muddy pawprints **everywhere.**

Ben's neighbours were having a party in their garden. "One of
the guests might be able to think of a good name for you," said
Ben. "Let's go and ask them."

"I'd rather look in the pond," thought the new puppy.

So he leaned over...

... and he leaned over a little bit more.

He didn't mean to fall in the pond, but...

Splosh!

That's just what he did.

He made muddy pawprints **everywhere.**

"We'd better go home and clean you up," said Ben.
"I'd rather go digging in the garden," thought the new puppy.

So he **dug**...

... and he **dug**...

... and he **dug**.

This time he found lots of things...

... a lost ring...

... an old spanner...

... and a toy car that
Ben had lost.

He didn't mean to bring
all that mud indoors, but...

Pitter Patter!

... that's just what he did.

He made muddy pawprints everywhere.

And he didn't mean to find a name for himself at last, but...
guess what? That's **just** what he did!

"You are the muckiest, muddiest, funniest puppy there ever was. There's only one name for you," laughed Ben.

"Muddypaws!"

Just One More Swim!

Big Bear stood up and sniffed the air, then lumbered out towards the water. Her cubs scampered after her, blinking at the dazzling world.

Big Bear padded across the ice. She stopped and dug a hole. She dipped in her paw and scooped out a fish!

The cubs did just what Big Bear did. One dug a hole. The other pounced on the cloud of white, and frightened off the fish. The cubs squabbled. They fought. They tackled each other and tumbled and rolled, over and over in the snow. They ran and raced on their snowshoe paws, and tummy-tobogganed on the ice. But then they stopped and stared.

"What is that?" they asked, gazing at the blue-green water.

Every morning, Big Bear coaxed her cubs a little farther towards the ocean. Then one day, Big Bear and her cubs slowly and carefully made their way to the water's edge. Big Bear gently slid into the icy sea.

"Come back!" squealed the cubs. But Big Bear swam out strongly to an island of ice in the waves.

The cubs waited, shivering on the thin ice. The water rippled. The cubs patted it – but it just wouldn't stay still. Then they put two paws in... and pulled them right back out again.

Big Bear called to her cubs to swim over to the island. "Come to me across the ocean," she urged. "You can do it! Swim!"

And the cubs did! Under the water they went, twisting and turning in the aquamarine sea. Then they dived down from on high, cutting through the waves, paddling with their paws. They splashed and somersaulted through the icy water. They paddled and swam until Big Bear insisted, "Come out now!"

The cubs pulled their weary bodies onto the ice. Then Big Bear led her cubs to where the juicy blueberries grew. The cubs ate and ate, until their muzzles and paws turned blue.

Big Bear sprawled on her back, enjoying the sunshine on her damp fur. But the cubs had other ideas. And, as they headed back towards the water one more time, Big Bear smiled as she heard their call...

"Just one more swim!"

Little Bear
Learns How

Little Bear and Grandma were eating breakfast.

"Grandma," asked Little Bear suddenly, "why do I have such a big nose?"

"To help you find food," Grandma told him.

"But I just looked around and I found these berries," argued Little Bear.

"Ah!" replied Grandma. "Food isn't always that easy to see."

Grandma led Little Bear down to the river.

"Can you see anything to eat?" she asked.

Little Bear shook his head.

"Can you smell anything?" Grandma added.

"Food," answered Little Bear.

"Then use your nose to find it," Grandma told him.

Little Bear followed his nose to some stones on the riverbank. He turned one over.

"A fish!" he laughed.

"Yummy!"

"Dinner," smiled Grandma. "Good work, Little Bear!"

"I love you, Grandma," Little Bear whispered in her ear.

"Grandma," asked Little Bear suddenly, "why do I have such sharp claws?"

"To help you find food," came the reply.

"But you told me I have my nose for that," said Little Bear, surprised.

"Ah!" said Grandma. "Sometimes your nose leads you to food, but you still have to work to get it."

She took Little Bear to the woods.

"Sniff the air!" she reminded him.

Little Bear started to follow his nose. He stopped at a fallen tree.

"I can smell food," Little Bear said.

"I still can't see it, but I know it's here."

"You'll need to use your claws," Grandma told him.

Little Bear dug his sharp claws into the bark. He broke off a small piece.

"Ants!" he laughed. "Delicious!"

"Lunch," smiled Grandma. "Good work, Little Bear!

"I love you, Grandma!"

Little Bear yelled.

"Grandma," asked Little Bear suddenly, "why do I have such a long tongue?"

"To help you find food," Grandma said at once.

"But you told me that I have my nose and claws to do that," said Little Bear, surprised.

"Sometimes the best food is hard to reach," Grandma told him.

She took Little Bear to a clearing.

"Smell the air," Grandma said.

Little Bear sniffed hard. He lifted his nose.

"Food!" he told Grandma. A huge bees' nest hung from a branch above him.

"I know what to do," laughed Little Bear.

"Look at me!"
he called.

He hooked the nest with his sharp claws, lifted it down and opened it up.

"Honey!" he smiled. "Mmmmm!"

"Supper," said Grandma. But Little Bear's big claws couldn't reach the food.

"So what are you going to do now?" asked Grandma.

"Use my long tongue," laughed Little Bear.

And that's just what he did.

"Brilliant, Little Bear!" laughed Grandma.
"How do you know so many things,
Grandma?" asked Little Bear suddenly.
"That's easy," Grandma smiled.
"When I was small,
I was curious...
just like you," she said.
"You ask so many
questions, you'll soon know
lots of things, too."

And she hugged Little
Bear tight
"Do you know I love
you, Grandma?" asked
Little Bear.
"I do!" answered Grandma.
She stroked Little Bear's
sticky head.
"And you know I love
you, too," she said.

81

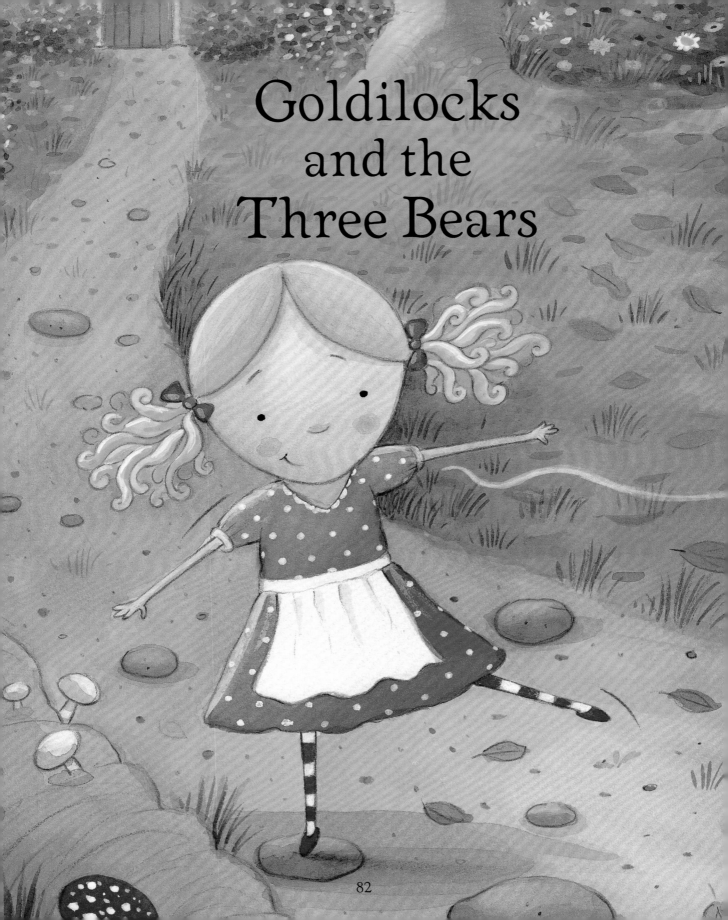

Goldilocks
and the
Three Bears

Once upon a time, Goldilocks was playing
in the woods near her home.

As she skipped along the pebbly path, her golden locks
bouncing, Goldilocks suddenly stopped and sniffed the air...

A yummy smell was coming from the middle of the woods.

RUMBLE RUMBLE!

As her tummy grumbled loudly, Goldilocks followed the delicious smell. She soon found herself in front of a little house.

"I wonder who lives here… " she said.

Goldilocks knocked loudly on the front door.

KNOCK, KNOCK, KNOCK…

But on the last KNOCK, the door swung open. There was no one at home.

Goldilocks saw three bowls of porridge on the kitchen table.

"I'm sure no one will mind if I have a little taste of this porridge," she told herself.

Goldilocks ate a spoonful of porridge from the biggest bowl. "Yuck!" she cried. "This porridge is far too cold!"

Goldilocks tried the medium-size bowl.
"Ouch!" she gasped. "This porridge is far too hot!"

Finally, Goldilocks took a little mouthful from the smallest bowl. "Mmmm!" she sighed. "This porridge is perfect!"
And she ate it all up.

Then, Goldilocks went into the living room for a rest. She saw a big chair, a medium-size chair and a tiny little chair.

Goldilocks climbed onto the biggest chair.

"This chair is too big!" she said.

Next, Goldilocks clambered onto the medium-size chair.

The cushions were very squashy.

"This chair is too soft!" she cried.

Then, Goldilocks tried the tiny chair.
"This chair is perfect!" beamed Goldilocks.
She was just getting comfortable, when...

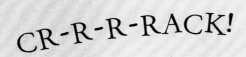

The chair broke into pieces.
"Oh, no!" Goldilocks gasped.
"Perhaps I should lie down instead."

Upstairs, Goldilocks found a big bed, a medium-size bed and a tiny little bed.

When she jumped on the big bed it was too hard. The medium-size bed was too soft for bouncing, and the little bed was...

"Perfect!" Goldilocks sighed happily.

And the little girl crawled under the covers and fell fast asleep.

ZZZzzzZZZzzzzzz

Meanwhile, three hungry bears returned to the little house. They had been for a walk while their hot porridge cooled down.

But the door was already open, and there were muddy footprints in the hall...

"Someone's been eating my porridge!" roared Daddy Bear.

"Someone's been eating my porridge too," growled Mummy Bear.
"Look!" squeaked Baby Bear. "My porridge has all gone!"

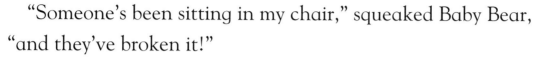

The three bears went into the living room.

"Someone's been sitting in my chair!" roared Daddy Bear.

"Someone's been sitting in my chair too," growled Mummy Bear.

"Someone's been sitting in my chair," squeaked Baby Bear, "and they've broken it!"

Suddenly, the three bears heard a noise coming from upstairs...

zzzzzzzzzzzzzzzZZ

"Someone's been sleeping in my bed!" roared Daddy Bear, as he stepped into the bedroom.

"Someone's been sleeping in my bed too," growled Mummy Bear, straightening the cover.

"Someone's been sleeping in my bed," squeaked Baby Bear, "and she's still there!"

Goldilocks woke up with a start and screamed.
The three bears watched in surprise as she
ran off through the forest as fast as her little legs
would carry her.

And guess what? The three bears never saw
Goldilocks again.

Little Bear's Close Encounter

Little Bear looked up at the stars.

"I wish I was an astronaut," he sighed.

Little Bear dreamed of exploring the world outside the window. He liked living in Emma's bedroom, but he sometimes wondered what it would be like to climb a mountain or go deep-sea diving. Most of all, Little Bear longed to meet an alien.

"Twinkle, twinkle, little bear," he sang to himself. "How I wonder what's up there."

"What are you looking at?" asked Monkey, coming over to join him at the window.

"I'm looking for spaceships," replied Little Bear, pressing his furry nose up against the window. "I want to meet a real alien," he explained.

"I wonder what they look like" said Monkey.

Little Bear told Monkey that Emma had a book all about aliens that they read together.

"They come in all shapes and sizes," he said.

"Are they scary?" asked Monkey.

"I hope not!" Little Bear replied.

Suddenly a big black shape appeared at the window, looming over the two friends.

"**Aaargh! An alien!**" cried Little Bear, jumping down from the windowsill.

"Do aliens meow?" asked Monkey.

"I'm not sure that they do," whispered Little Bear.

"Do aliens purr?" asked Monkey.

"It didn't say anything about purring in Emma's book," said Little Bear, feeling a little braver.

"Do aliens have whiskers and a long furry tail?" giggled Monkey.

"Definitely not!" said Little Bear, beginning to feel rather foolish.

Little Bear and Monkey climbed back onto the windowsill. Was it an alien? No it was Emma's cat, Sooty.

"**Meow!**" said Sooty.

Little Bear decided that he'd had enough excitement for one night.

"Perhaps I don't want to meet an alien, after all," he chuckled.

Huggle Buggle Bear

Where, oh where is **Huggle Buggle** Bear?
I can't find him anywhere!
He always hides when it's time for bed.
He is such a **funny** bear!

Is he snacking on toast and honey,
Making crumbs with **Babbity Bunny?**

No!
He isn't with
Babbity Bunny.

It's way past Huggle Buggle's bedtime
And I'm feeling very cross.
I can't go to bed without him.
I hope he isn't lost!

Where, oh where is Huggle Buggle Bear?
I can't find him anywhere!
He always hides when it's time for bed.
He is such a silly bear!

Is he bouncing on his belly,
On the sofa with Ellie Nellie?

No!
He isn't bouncing with
Ellie Nellie.
And he isn't snacking with
Babbity Bunny.

It's way past **Huggle Buggle's** bedtime
And I'm feeling very sleepy.
I can't go to bed without him,
It's much too dark and creepy.
Where, oh where is **Huggle Buggle** Bear?
I can't find him anywhere!
He always hides when it's time for bed.
He is such a **naughty** bear!

Is he making lots of noise
With Woolly Lamb and the other toys?

No!
He isn't playing with
Woolly Lamb.
He isn't bouncing with
Ellie Nellie.
He isn't snacking with
Babbity Bunny.

It's way past **Huggle Buggle's** bedtime
And now I'm feeling worried.
I can't go to bed without him.
That would be really horrid.

Where, oh where is **Huggle Buggle** Bear?
I can't find him anywhere!
He always hides when it's time for bed.
He is such a **bothersome** bear.

Is he splashing in the tub,
Blowing bubbles with Rubadub?

No!

He isn't splashing with
Rubadub.
He isn't playing with
Woolly Lamb.
He isn't bouncing with
Ellie Nellie.
He isn't snacking with
Babbity Bunny.

It's way past Huggle Buggle's bedtime
And now I'm feeling sad.
I don't want to go to bed without him,
But I think I better had...

I know where...
there's Huggle Buggle Bear!
And all the other toys.
I think they must be fast asleep,
So, **sssh!** Don't make a noise!

Night-night!

The Pied Piper of Hamelin

The town of Hamelin was overrun by rats.

One day, a stranger came to see the mayor. "I will rid your town of rats if you pay me one hundred gold coins," he said.

The mayor agreed and so the stranger began to play an enchanting tune on a pipe. The rats followed the piper, who led them into a river where they drowned. But when the piper went to ask for his money, the mayor refused to pay.

The next day, the piper returned and played his tune again. This time it was not rats that followed him, but children.

"When you pay me what you owe, I will return the children," he told the mayor.

The people of Hamelin were **furious**. They all marched to the town hall to see the mayor.

"Pay the piper what he is owed," they shouted.

The mayor paid the piper, and the children were returned to their parents. The people of Hamelin chose a new mayor and, from then on, Hamelin thrived.

The Prince and the Peasant

Once there was a young prince who wanted to go exploring.
By chance, he met a peasant boy who looked exactly like him.
He realized that if they swapped clothes he would get his wish.

The peasant boy agreed and, as soon as they swapped, the
prince felt a hand on his shoulder. "There you are, lad,"
said a **gruff** voice.

The prince was led away and put to work in a field. It
was hard work and by the time he had finished he was very
hungry. But all he got for his supper was a thin soup and a
crust of bread.

The next day, the prince and the boy changed back
into their own clothes. "When I am king, I promise
to make sure that nobody goes hungry,"
he told the boy.

The prince grew up and, when he
was king, he did not forget
his promise.

The Wedding of Mrs Fox

Mrs Fox was feeling very sad because her husband had died.

"Don't be so sad," said her maid, who was a cat. "You'll soon find someone else to marry." But Mrs Fox wasn't so sure.

"I'll never find another husband as good as Mr Fox," she sighed. "He had such fine **red stockings** and such a lovely **pointed mouth**."

One day, the maid knocked on Mrs Fox's door.

"Here's Mr Badger to see you," she said. And in came Mr Badger. Mrs Fox could not deny that he had lovely black and white stripes, but he did not have fine red stockings or a lovely pointed mouth. So, when he asked Mrs Fox to be his wife, she turned him down.

One day, the maid knocked on Mrs Fox's door again. "Here's Mr Squirrel to see you," she said. And in came Mr Squirrel. Mrs Fox admired Mr Squirrel's lovely bushy tail, but he did not have fine red stockings or a lovely pointed mouth.

So when he begged her to marry him, Mrs Fox said that she would rather not.

One day, the maid knocked on Mrs Fox's door yet again. "Here's Mr Mouse to see you," she said. And in came Mr Mouse.

Mrs Fox had to admit that he did have a rather attractive pointed mouth, but no fine red stockings. So when he popped the question, Mrs Fox was flattered, but still refused him.

One day, the maid knocked on Mrs Fox's door yet again. "There's a young man to see you," she said. And in came a handsome fox. He had a beautiful pointed mouth, and very fine red stockings. The handsome fox came to visit Mrs Fox every day, and they fell in love.

"Mrs Fox, will you be my bride?" asked the handsome fox.

"Yes!" replied Mrs Fox. And they lived happily ever after.

Little Brother
and
Little Sister

Once upon a time, there was a little brother and a little sister who lived with their stepmother who was very cruel to them.

One night, the brother and sister decided to run away. So the two children ran out into the forest, curled up in the hollow of a tree and fell asleep.

Their stepmother, who was really a wicked **witch**, followed the children. When she found them asleep, she put a curse on a nearby stream knowing that they would drink from it.

The next morning, the two children bent down to drink from the stream. But the stream whispered a warning:

"Brother and sister, although my water's clear, do not drink it, or you'll become a deer." The little sister listened to the warning, but her brother could not resist taking a drink.

He was **transformed** into a deer.

"Don't worry, I'll look after you," said the kind sister, and she led the little deer into the woods.

They found a wooden hut in a clearing and, as it was empty, they lived there happily for a long time.

But one spring, a king was hunting in the forest. **Thwack!** He shot the deer with an arrow. The wounded deer limped back to his sister, now a beautiful woman. The king followed, and when he saw the sister he lost his heart to her, and the two were married. The deer was nursed back to health and stayed with his sister and the king.

After all this time, the brother and sister had almost forgotten about their wicked stepmother, but she had not forgotten them. She knew where they were and still wanted to harm them.

When the king and queen's first child was born, the stepmother **crept** into the palace grounds to try and steal it. The king's hunting dogs sniffed out the wicked woman and chased her away. They were so fierce that the wicked witch didn't stop running until she had left the kingdom. Once the witch was gone, her spell was broken and the brother returned to his human form.

The witch never bothered them again.

Seven Ravens

Once there lived a man and a woman who had seven sons, but longed for a daughter. When their eighth child was a girl, they were very happy. At last their wish had come true.

The beautiful baby girl was a thirsty little thing, so the seven sons were sent out to the well to fetch water.

"Take this silver cup and fill it for the baby," said their mother. But the silver cup fell into the well with a **splash!** The boys were too frightened to go home.

When they didn't return, their father cursed them. "May those lazy good-for-nothing boys become ravens!" he shouted. As soon as the words left his mouth, he saw seven ravens flying off into the distance. Although he regretted his words, it was too late to undo his curse.

When the little girl grew older, her sad mother told her all about her seven lost brothers. The brave girl vowed to find them and bring them home.

She set off, taking her mother's ring as a keepsake, and searched the world over. **"Where are my seven brothers?"** she called up to the heavens.

The stars could see that the poor girl was in

despair and took pity on her. They sent down a magical key and, as the girl picked it up, she heard these words:

"Follow our light to a mountain of glass,
You'll find your raven brothers at last."

After walking for many days, the young girl finally reached the glass mountain. Using the key she entered a crystal cave and, although nobody was there, she noticed seven little plates and cups laid out with food and drink ready for their return.

Being very hungry, she took a bite from each plate and a sip from each cup. Her ring fell into the last cup, but before she could pick it up again she heard the swish of wings. She hid behind a door and watched seven ravens swoop down.

Each raven noticed that some of their food and drink was missing. Then the last raven found the ring in his cup and recognized it as his mother's.

"If only our little sister has come to find us," he exclaimed, "for then we could return home with her."

On hearing this, their brave little sister jumped out from behind the door. As soon as they saw her, the ravens turned back into their human form.

They returned home to a huge celebration and lived happily ever after.

The Elves
and the
Shoemaker

Once upon a time, a shoemaker lived with his wife above
his workshop.

The shoemaker was a good man, and he worked hard, but he
was very poor. The day came when he had only enough leather
to make one pair of shoes.

He cut out the leather and then left it on his workbench.

"I will be able to make a better pair of shoes after I've had a
good night's sleep," he told his wife as they went upstairs.

The next morning, the shoemaker went downstairs. **What a surprise he had!** On his workbench, where the leather had been, there was a **brand-new pair of shoes**. They were neatly and perfectly made, with not a stitch out of place.

"These shoes are masterpieces!" the shoemaker exclaimed to his wife. He put them in the window, hoping someone would come and buy them.

Sure enough, a finely dressed young man soon entered the workshop to try on the shoes. They fitted perfectly, and they were so handsome that the man happily paid a high price for them.

With the money, the shoemaker was able to buy enough leather to make two new pairs of shoes.

By the time he returned to his shop, he was tired, so he cut out the leather and left it on his workbench. Then he went upstairs to bed.

The next morning, the shoemaker had
another surprise! There on the workbench were
TWO new pairs of shoes! They were
even more beautiful than the first pair, and
were just as perfectly made.

The shoemaker put them in the window, and
before lunchtime he had sold both pairs for a very good price.

Now he had enough money to buy leather for four pairs of shoes.

Once again, he cut out the
leather, left it on his workbench
and went upstairs to bed.

And once again, he came
down the next morning to find
beautiful shoes, all made up and
perfectly stitched.

124

The same thing happened every day for weeks. The shoes were appearing as if by magic.

"Let's try and find out who's been making them tonight," his wife suggested.

So that night, the shoemaker left some leather, all cut out and ready to sew, on his workbench as usual.

Then, instead of going to bed, he and his wife hid behind a curtain at the back of the shop.

There they waited... and waited... and waited.

The shoemaker and his wife were just about to go to bed when, at the stroke of midnight, the shop door opened, and in danced two tiny elves! They skipped up to the workbench, and quickly began sewing the leather into fine new shoes. As they worked, they sang,

"We will sew and we will stitch,

To help the shoemaker grow rich!"

Soon the shoes were finished and the little elves leapt off the workbench and danced out of the shop.

"Those kind elves have helped us," said the shoemaker, astonished. "We must repay them."

"Did you see how thin their clothes were?" his wife asked. "And their little feet were bare! Those poor little men must be freezing."

"Let's make some warm clothes for the elves, to show how grateful we are," said the shoemaker.

The next day, the shoemaker's wife knitted two
cosy woollen jackets... two tiny scarves... and two
pairs of warm trousers.

The shoemaker used his finest leather to make
two little pairs of boots.

That night, instead of leaving leather on his workbench, the shoemaker left the clothes, all wrapped up in shiny paper and ribbons. Then he and his wife hid behind the curtain to wait.

At the stroke of midnight, the shop door opened, and in came the little elves.

They hopped up onto the workbench and saw the presents that had been left for them.

They opened the parcels at once, and in the twinkling of an eye, they had dressed in their brand-new clothes.

They knew that the presents were the shoemaker's way of saying thank you, and they did a happy dance together, singing,

"Now the shoemaker's grown rich,

There's no need to sew and stitch."

Then they hopped off the workbench and scurried out of the door.

The shoemaker and his wife never saw the little elves again. But their troubles were over, and they had a good and happy life together for many long years.

Alice
and the
White Rabbit

One day, Alice was sitting beside a river with her sister, when something curious happened. A white Rabbit with pink eyes ran past.

"Oh, dear! Oh, dear! I shall be too late," he said. Then he took a watch out of his vest pocket and hurried on.

Alice followed the Rabbit down a large rabbit hole. The rabbit hole went straight on like a tunnel for some way, and then dipped so suddenly she found herself falling **down...**

"I must be getting near the centre of the Earth," Alice thought to herself. **Down, down, down** Alice kept falling.

Suddenly she landed in a heap at the bottom. When she got up she found herself in a long hall, lined with doors. At the end was a little three-legged glass table. There was nothing on it but a tiny golden key. Alice tried the key in all the doors, but it wouldn't open any of them. Then she noticed a low curtain she had not seen before. Behind it was a tiny door.

She turned the key in the lock and it opened. The door led into a beautiful garden, but Alice could not even get her head through

the doorway. She went back to the table and saw a little bottle labelled **"DRINK ME!"**

Once she was sure it wasn't poison, Alice drank it and shrank. But she remembered that she had left the key on the table. Alice didn't know what to do. Then she saw a cake marked **"EAT ME!"**

Alice ate it and began to grow. Soon she was so large her head touched the ceiling!

Alice began to cry. She was wondering what to do, when who should come along but the white Rabbit. He was carrying a pair of white gloves and a large fan.

"If you please, sir..." began Alice.

The Rabbit dropped the gloves and fan, and scurried away.

"How strange everything is today," said Alice, picking up the gloves and the fan. "I'm not myself at all." Then she began fanning herself as she wondered who she might be instead.

After a while, Alice looked down at her hands. She was surprised to see that she had put on one of the Rabbit's little white gloves.

"I must be growing smaller again," she thought.

Alice realized that it was the fan that was making her shrink, so she dropped it quickly and ran to the door. Suddenly, she remembered that the key was still on the table.

"Drat," she said. "Things can't possibly get any worse." But she was wrong. SPLASH! She fell into her sea of tears.

"I wish I hadn't cried so much!" wailed Alice.

Just then, she heard something splashing. It was a Mouse.

"Mouse, do you know the way out of this pool?" asked Alice.

The Mouse didn't reply.

"Perhaps he speaks French," thought Alice. So she began again. "Où est mon chat?" which was the first sentence in her French book and meant "Where is my cat?"

The Mouse leaped out of the water in fright.

"I'm sorry!" cried Alice. "I didn't mean to scare you."

"Come ashore," said the Mouse. "I'll tell you why cats frighten me."

By this time the pool was crowded with birds and animals. There was a Duck, a Dodo, a Parrot, an Eaglet and other curious creatures, too. Together, they all swam to the shore.

The birds and animals were dripping wet.

"Let's have a race," said the Dodo. "It will help us to dry off." And he began to mark out a course.

Then, when everyone was dotted along the course, they began starting and stopping whenever they felt like it. It was impossible to tell when the race was over, but after half an hour they were all very dry.

"But who won the race?" asked the Mouse.

"Everyone," said the Dodo. "Alice will give out prizes." So Alice handed around some candy she had in her pocket.

"But she must have a prize, too," said the Mouse.

"What else do you have in your pocket?" asked the Dodo.

Alice handed over a thimble, and he gave it back to her saying, "I beg you to accept this thimble."

Alice accepted as solemnly as she could, and then they all sat down to hear the Mouse's tale. But Alice was so tired, she just couldn't concentrate, and the Mouse stomped away in a huff!

"I wish my cat, Dinah, were here," said Alice. "She'd soon fetch him back."

Then she tried to tell everyone about Dinah – but they were scared of cats too, and ran away. Poor Alice was alone again.

Benji's New Friends

Benji the bear sat on the end of the bed, feeling a little bit lonely. He was new here and he hadn't seen anyone else in the bedroom.

He watched a moonbeam slip through a gap in the curtains and slide across the bed.

"I wish that I had someone to play with," he whispered.

"Did I hear someone say they wanted to play?" asked a voice. The lid of the toy box flew open, and out climbed a dangly legged, spotty horse.

"Hi, I'm Cleo... and I love to play!"

Boing! Boing!

Cleo jumped onto the bed and began to bounce up and down.

"Where did you come from?" she asked.

"From the birthday party," replied Benji. "I was a present."

"Did someone mention a party?" A friendly looking monkey poked his head around the curtain. "Why weren't Rosie and I invited?"

A floppy-eared rabbit appeared beside him.

"Max and I love parties!" Rosie the rabbit told Benji. "And so does Humph."

"Who's Humph?" asked Benji.

A loud yawn came from inside a box. Then a bright-blue hippo slowly lifted his head.

"I am!" he said. "A party..." he continued thoughtfully. "That means food. And I'm hungry! Is there anything left to eat?"

"I think there are some cakes in the kitchen," replied Benji, "but do you think we should?"

But Humph was already through the door!

"Oh!" said Benji. "Should we go after him?"

Benji was bumping down the stairs after Humph when Cleo zoomed past.

"This is fun!" she neighed.

"Wait for me!" called Benji. In the kitchen, Humph was about to take a bite out of a leftover cupcake with a candle in it.

The candle was already halfway into Humph's mouth. Benji grabbed it just in time.

"Excuse me," he explained, "but you aren't meant to eat that bit."

"Thanks, Benji. You're smart. I wish I knew things like that," grumbled Humph.

Before Benji could explain about the candle, he heard Rosie yell loudly. Benji raced back up to the bedroom where he found Rosie hiding under the bed. She had seen a big owl swoop past the window and it had given her quite a fright.

"Don't worry," said Benji, and he explained to everyone that owls never came inside people's houses and that they were all quite safe.

"Benji, will you always be here to look after us?" Cleo asked him. Benji gave a tiny little smile. It was nice to feel wanted. "Of course," he replied.

Humph was tired from their adventure. "How am I going to sleep when I'm so hungry?" he sniffed, settling back down on the bed.

Cleo and Rosie giggled. They danced around on the bed. Max joined in.

"Why don't we play in the garden tomorrow?" Rosie suggested.

"What's your garden like?" asked Benji.

"I'll show you," said Cleo, and she helped Benji up to have a look out of the window.

"Wow!" he said. "It looks really exciting. Are you going to play in the garden, Humph?"

"Humph!" said Humph sleepily. "It's such a long way to the garden. I might just have a little nap instead."

Benji smiled at his new sleepy friend.

Cleo jumped back onto the bed and started to bounce. Benji looked up at the moon. He had a feeling that he wouldn't be lonely any more.

"I wish that tomorrow will be as much fun as today," he whispered.

Then Benji turned to his new friends, took a huge leap and began to bounce on the bed.

"Here's to friends!" he laughed.

The Ugly Duckling

It was a warm summer's day and Mummy Duck wriggled excitedly on her nest. She could hear a tapping noise. Tap, tap, tap, tap!

"Quick! Quack! Quick!"

Mummy Duck called to the other ducks. "My eggs are hatching. Come and see!"

One by one, the eggs hatched and out popped six chirpy little ducklings.

"Ahhhh!" the other ducks sighed. "What sweet little ducklings!" Mummy Duck beamed with pride.

But the biggest egg of all still hadn't opened. Mummy Duck was sure she had only laid six eggs...

Craaaaaaaaaaaaack!

Just then the final egg burst open.

"Oh!" gasped Mummy Duck.

The last duckling wasn't little, yellow or cute. He was enormous, grey and, well, ugly.

"What an ugly duckling!" quacked an old duck.

"He's not ugly!" said Mummy Duck protectively. "He's special."

142

The next day, Mummy Duck took all her little ducks to the farmyard, to meet the other animals. The six yellow ducklings proudly puffed out their pretty feathers.

"Ah," sighed the animals, "what lovely ducklings."

The ugly duckling waddled forward.

"Hello," he said quietly.

Everyone turned to stare at him.

"He's so GREY!" neighed the horse.

"He's so CLUMSY!" mooed the cow.

"He's so BIG!" squawked the hen.

Large teardrops rolled down the ugly duckling's long, black beak. He felt all alone.

"Nobody wants me," he whispered. "I'd be better off swimming away."

The poor little duckling waddled sadly across the meadow, leaving the farm and his family far behind him.

Soon the ugly duckling arrived at a river, where some geese were diving for food.

"Excuse me," the ugly duckling began bravely, "have you seen any ducklings like me?"

"No. You're the strangest looking duckling we've ever seen," the geese honked.

So the ugly duckling waddled on. He was getting very tired.

As darkness fell, he crept inside an old barn, looking for a place to rest.

"May I stay here?"

he asked the animals inside.

"Can you lay eggs?"

clucked a hen.

"No," said the ugly duckling sadly.

"Can you catch mice?"

purred a cat.

"I don't think so," said the ugly duckling.

"Then you're no use here!" the cat hissed.

The ugly duckling quickly waddled away. He kept going until he came to a large lake.

"If nobody wants me, then I'll just hide here forever," he sniffed sadly.

"Ribbit!" croaked a frog. "What a funny-looking duckling!"

Autumn came and the leaves turned gold.

One evening, just as the sun was setting, the ugly duckling saw a flock of beautiful white birds flying gracefully across the sky.

"I wish I looked like them," he sighed.

All through the long winter, the ugly duckling hid in the reeds, ashamed to show his face.

When the first rays of warm spring sunshine arrived, the ugly duckling peered out of his hiding place. A graceful swan paddled by him, and he backed away, afraid he would be teased.

But to the ugly duckling's surprise, the swan swam up to him.

"Why are you hiding here?" asked the swan, kindly. "Join the rest of us."

The ugly duckling was shocked. Surely the swan must be talking to someone else.

But then he caught sight of his reflection in the lake.

He stared and gasped in amazement. His grey feathers were now snowy white!

"I'm a swan!" the ugly duckling cried happily.

Just then a family of six young
ducks waddled along the riverbank
with their mother.

"Look at that beautiful swan!"
they quacked.

Mummy Duck recognized her little ugly duckling at once.
"I always knew he was special," she quacked.

The ugly duckling ruffled his beautiful white feathers, turned away and proudly paddled after his new friend.

Thank You for Being My Friend

It was a dark night. In the bedroom, nothing stirred. Nothing except a heap of bright wrapping paper on the end of the bed.

The paper **rustled**.

It **crackled**.

It **shook**.

And then out jumped a toy horse.

"Hello!" said the horse. "I'm Cleo."

But there was no answer. Cleo trotted across the bed.

"Where is everybody?"
she wondered,
"I don't like the dark and... Oof!"

Cleo t u m b l e d

onto the floor.

There were strange shapes in the dark.
"I'm scared," shivered Cleo. **"I can see monsters!"**

There was a **thin monster**...
a **cuddly monster**...
a **tall square monster**...
And a **monster with no head!**

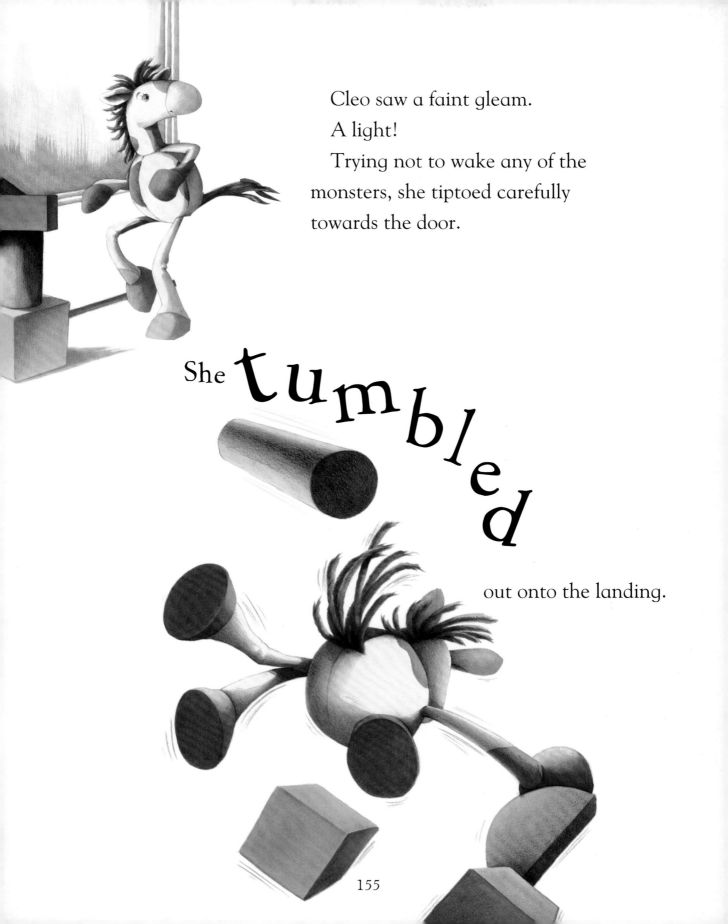

Cleo saw a faint gleam.
A light!
Trying not to wake any of the monsters, she tiptoed carefully towards the door.

She tumbled

out onto the landing.

155

"Oh," said Cleo,
"it's only the moon." Suddenly
a cloud slid over the moon and
everything went dark.

And then something
downstairs went

BONG!

BONG!

Cleo nearly jumped out of her skin.
 "Another monster!" she whinnied.

BONG!

BONG!

"Help!"
neighed Cleo.

Cleo spun on her hooves and galloped back the way she had come.

Cleo trotted into the bedroom and tripped over something on the floor.

"Ugh," groaned the Thing drowsily.

"Who... who are you?"

"I'm C-Cleo," muttered Cleo.

"P-please don't eat me up!"

Then the moon came out again and Cleo saw that the Thing was a fluffy yellow duck.

"I'm Daphne," smiled the duck.

"And why would I want to eat you?"

Cleo told Daphne all about the monsters.

"The monsters won't hurt you," said Daphne.

"Promise?" asked Cleo with a big yawn. "Promise," said Daphne kindly. "Why don't you snuggle down with me?"

"You won't go, will you?" said Cleo.

"No. You're safe now. Good night," said Daphne.

Good night!

The next morning, Cleo peeped out from under Daphne's wing.
She blinked in the bright sunlight.

"Morning, sleepyhead," quacked Daphne. "Come and meet
all the monsters!"

Cleo shot back under Daphne's wing.

"Don't worry," laughed Daphne.

"They won't eat
you, I promised,
remember."

The thin monster was...
a lamp!  
The cuddly monster was...
a pile of cushions!
The tall square monster was...
a wardrobe!  
And the headless monster was...
a dressing gown!

And

the
one
that
chased
Cleo
was...

The grandfather clock!

Tick

Tock

Tick

Tock

"I've been really silly," smiled Cleo.
"No, you haven't," said Daphne.
"Lots of things look more
scary in the dark."

"I don't think I'll be scared any more," said Cleo. "Now that you're my friend."

The Tortoise and the Hare

Once upon a time, there was a hare who was always boasting about how fast he was.

"I," he would say, puffing out his chest and flexing his legs, "am the **speediest** animal in the forest. I have never been beaten. I challenge anyone to try and beat me."

And, of course, nobody took up the challenge because he was right – he was the fastest animal in the forest.

The animals who lived in the forest were becoming tired of Hare's bragging, until one day, much to everyone's surprise, after Hare had been boasting even more than normal,

"Okay, Hare. I'll race you," Tortoise said.

"**Whaaaaat?**" laughed Hare. "You've got to be joking. Tortoise, you're the slowest animal in the forest. I'll run circles around you."

"You might be fast," replied Tortoise, "but speed isn't everything. Why don't we have a race? You can keep your boasting until you actually beat me."

"Speed might not be everything but it sure helps in a race," laughed Hare. He laughed so much that he fell to his knees and thumped the floor with his fist. He'd never heard of anything so ridiculous in his life.

That night, while the forest animals prepared the course, Tortoise went to bed early so he'd have a lot of energy for the race. Hare, meanwhile, stayed up late boxing with his friends. He knew he could beat the slow tortoise even if he was tired.

There was a buzz of **excitement** in the forest the next morning. No one had heard of Hare ever losing a race so this was going to be quite an event! Everyone gathered at the starting line to watch the race begin. All the forest animals wanted Tortoise to win, but deep down they knew that Hare was the fastest.

Tortoise was already at the starting line, trying his best to look confident. He looked around for Hare, who had just arrived and was making his way to the starting line. He strutted towards Tortoise with his chest puffed out proudly.

The crowd fell silent…

"On your marks, get set… GO!" cried the starting fox.

Hare flew off at high speed but Tortoise trudged behind much more slooooooowly.

Hare decided to take a quick look behind to see where the slow tortoise was. When he saw that Tortoise was far, far away, he decided to stop for breakfast. He feasted on some juicy carrots. Then he lay on his back, fiddled with his ears and yawned.

"This is just too easy," he said, loud enough for just about all the animals in the forest to hear. "I think I'll have forty winks and catch up with him later." Soon he was snoring happily away.

ZZZZZZZZ!

Tortoise got to where Hare was lying, fast asleep. "Maybe I should wake him?" he thought, as he plodded past Hare. "No, I'm sure Hare wouldn't like that. He will wake up soon enough and come whizzing by."

And so Tortoise plodded on and on and on. Hare slept, on and on and on. In Hare's dreams, all the forest animals cheered and clapped as he streamed past the finish line.

The sun began to sink, still Tortoise plodded on, and still Hare slept. The sun was just about to set when Hare awoke with a jolt.

He could just see Tortoise in the distance, plodding slowly and carefully towards the finish line.

"Noooooooo!" cried Hare. He leapt to his feet and charged towards the finish.

He ran as fast as his legs could carry him, but it just wasn't fast enough — he was too late!

Tortoise was over the line before him. Hare had been beaten fair and square.

Tortoise was a hero, and all the forest animals were there to cheer him.

After that, if anyone heard Hare boasting about how fast he could run, they reminded him about the day that Tortoise had beaten him.

"Slow and steady won the race," they would say.

And all Hare could do was smile and shrug because, after all, they were absolutely right.

Tom Thumb

There was once a poor couple who had no children and longed for a son of their own.

One day, an old beggar man passed by their house. Although the poor couple had little enough for themselves, they invited him in to eat and rest.

"Where are your children?" asked the beggar.

"We don't have any," sighed the man. "We would dearly love a son, even if he were no bigger than my thumb."

Little did the unhappy couple realize that their guest had magical powers. He rewarded their kindness by granting their wish to have a son, even a very tiny one.

The next morning, when the couple came downstairs to breakfast, they found a tiny boy waiting for them on the table.

He was no bigger than the man's thumb, and so his delighted parents named him Tom Thumb.

Tom had an unstoppable sense of adventure. "You are only small and the world is a dangerous place," warned his mother.

But Tom was too busy having fun to listen.

One day, Tom was playing by the river. He fell in and got eaten by a fish. The fish was caught and taken to the king's chef. Being a quick-thinking lad, Tom managed to crawl out of the fish. The chef was very shocked to see a tiny boy climbing out from the king's dinner!

Thinking the chef might harm him, Tom ran away. He hid in a mouse hole and soon made friends with the mouse who lived there.

"Climb onto my back," said the mouse. And Tom rode through the palace on the mouse's back, until he found himself in the throne room.

"My goodness!" exclaimed the king. "What have we here?"

Tom sang a song and danced for the king, who was delighted with the tiny boy and asked him to come and live at the palace. When the king heard that Tom had parents who would be missing him, he sent for the poor couple and let them live in a cottage of their own in the royal grounds. Tom entertained the king and all his courtiers, and he could visit his parents whenever he liked.

Tom and his parents lived happily ever after.

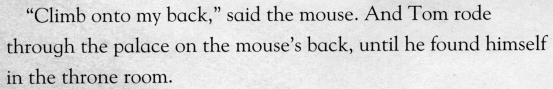

The Magic Mirror

There was once a magic mirror that could show the future.

One day, a courtier to the prince looked in the magic mirror and was **horrified** to see the prince being robbed. He had seen the face of the robber quite clearly, so the courtier decided to be on the lookout for this scoundrel.

A few days later, the courtier was walking through a forest with the prince when he saw the rogue in the mirror coming towards them.

"Look out, your majesty!" he shouted, as the man ran towards them.

The man from the mirror rushed at the prince, knocking him sideways. Just seconds later, a tree came crashing down, narrowly missing them all.

Everything the courtier had seen in the mirror had come true – but not in the way he had expected. The man he saw was not a robber after all. He was pushing the prince away from the falling tree.

The so-called robber had saved the prince's life!

From then on, the courtier looked at things a lot more carefully, and stopped jumping to conclusions.

The Princess
and the Pea

Once upon a time, there was a lonely
prince. He lived in a big castle with
beautiful rooms and a pretty garden. But
he wasn't happy because he didn't have
someone special to share them with.

"If only I could find a lovely princess
to marry," sighed the prince.

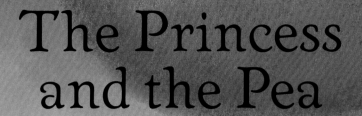

The king and queen did their best to help. They held balls so the prince could meet princesses from all the nearby kingdoms.

The prince danced with tall princesses and small princesses. He talked to LOUD princesses and proud princesses.

He met all kinds of princesses... but none of them were quite right.

After a while, the king and queen
ran out of princesses for their son
to meet.

"Maybe it's time you went looking
for a bride," suggested the queen.

So the prince packed a bag, saddled
his horse and waved goodbye to the
king and queen.

The prince travelled far and wide, and searched high and low for the princess of his dreams Along the way, he met lots of pretty princesses.

Princess Grace loved to dance, but her twirling made the prince dizzy.

Princess Ginger loved to cook, but her cakes made the prince chubby.

Princess Flora loved to smell as pretty as a flower, but her perfume made the prince sneezy.

ATCHOOOO!

Maybe I'm just too fussy, thought the prince. But in his heart, he knew he hadn't met the princess of his dreams. So he headed back to the castle.

When he got home, the king and queen greeted the prince happily.

"I haven't found a princess yet," he sniffed sadly. "I guess I never will."

"Don't be silly," said the queen, "the right girl will come along soon."

That night, there was a terrible storm. Thunder boomed so loudly that it rattled the castle's windows. Lightning shook the table as the prince and his parents sat down to eat their dinner. The prince was just about to help himself to dinner when, suddenly, they all heard a loud...

RAT-A-TAT-TAT!

Someone was knocking on the door!

"Who could be visiting us on a night like this?" asked the queen. The prince opened the door and found a very wet girl stood there. Raindrops ran down her muddy cloak, making a puddle at her feet.

The girl pushed back
her hood and wild curls
tumbled out.

"Hello," she said with a smile. "I got lost on my way home
and wondered if I could stay here for the night. My name is
Princess Polly."

She didn't look much like a princess. But princes must always
be polite, so he invited her inside.

Soon the princess was warm and dry.

All night long, rain fell plippety plop, plippety plop on the castle roof. But the prince hardly noticed, because he was too busy talking to Princess Polly.

She was pretty and funny and kind. Princess Polly was everything the prince had hoped to find in a princess.

By the end of the evening, the prince had fallen in love!

But the queen wanted to be sure that the girl really was a princess.

The queen told the servants to pile a bed high with mattresses. They heaved one on top of another until they had no more mattresses left. Then they placed a pillow and blanket right at the top.

Underneath the mattress at the very bottom, the queen placed a teeny, tiny pea.

Only a real princess would be able to feel something so small through all those mattresses!

When the queen showed Princess Polly to her bedroom, the girl gazed up at the tower of mattresses but didn't say anything. She was just grateful to have a bed for the evening.

"Goodnight," said Princess Polly.

"Sleep tight," whispered the queen.

Then Princess Polly changed into her nightgown and climbed to the top of the pile of mattresses, and snuggled under the blanket.

The next morning,
Princess Polly came down
to breakfast with dark
circles under her eyes.

She let out a great
big YAWN.

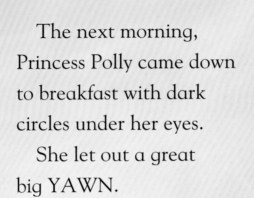

"How did you sleep, my
dear?" asked the queen.

Princess Polly burst
into tears.

"I'm afraid I couldn't
sleep a wink. There was
something lumpy in my
bed. It kept me awake
all night long!"

To Princess Polly's surprise, the queen clapped her hands with delight.

"She is a real princess!" the queen cried. The prince was overjoyed. "Will you marry me, Princess Polly?" he asked.

"Yes!" squealed the princess.
And they all lived happily ever after!

Jack and Jill

Jack and Jill went up the hill
To fetch a pail of water;
Jack fell down and broke his crown,
And Jill came tumbling after.
Up Jack got, and home did trot
As fast as he could caper;
He went to bed, to mend his head,
With vinegar and brown paper.

The Grand Old Duke of York

The grand old Duke of York,
He had ten thousand men,
He marched them up to the top of the hill,
And he marched them down again.
When they were up, they were up,
And when they were down, they were down,
And when they were only half way up,
They were neither up nor down.

Three Blind Mice

Three blind mice, three blind mice,
See how they run, see how they run!
They all ran after the farmer's wife,
Who cut off their tails with a carving knife.
Did you ever see such a thing in your life
As three blind mice?

Little Miss Muffet

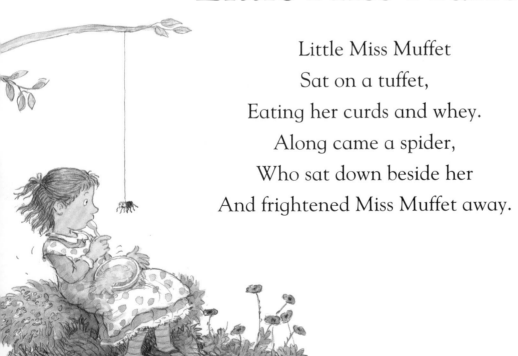

Little Miss Muffet
Sat on a tuffet,
Eating her curds and whey.
Along came a spider,
Who sat down beside her
And frightened Miss Muffet away.

Sail Away

Sail away, for a year and a day,
To a land where dreams come true,
Lit by the moon and a blanket of stars,
Across the ocean blue.

We'll drift through silver waters
To lands we've never seen
In daylight hours, where chocolate flowers
Will taste just like a dream.

Where clouds are cotton candy,
And the sky is always blue.
What busy night-time travelling,
Will you come with us too?

Incy Wincy Spider

Incy Wincy Spider
Climbed up the spout,
Down came the rain
And washed the spider out.
Out came the sun
And dried up all the rain,
Incy Wincy Spider
Climbed up the spout again.

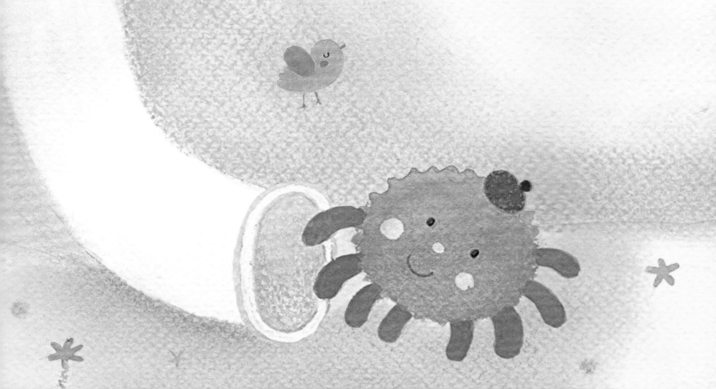

Mary Had a Little Lamb

Mary had a little lamb,
Whose fleece was white as snow.
And everywhere that Mary went,
The lamb was sure to go.
It followed her to school one day,
Which was against the rules.
It made the children laugh and play,
To see a lamb at school.

Little Bo-Peep

Little Bo-Peep has lost her sheep,
And doesn't know where to find them;
Leave them alone,
And they'll come home,
Bringing their tails behind them.

What Are
Little Girls Made Of?

What are little girls made of?
What are little girls made of?
Sugar and spice,
And all things nice,
That's what little girls are made of.

What Are
Little Boys Made Of?

What are little boys made of?
What are little boys made of?
Slugs and snails,
And puppy-dogs' tails,
That's what little boys are made of.

Hey Diddle Diddle

Hey diddle diddle, the cat and the fiddle,
The cow jumped over the moon.
The little dog laughed to see such fun
And the dish ran away with the spoon!

The Queen of Hearts

The Queen of Hearts, she made some tarts
All on a summer's day.
The Knave of Hearts, he stole the tarts
And took them clean away.
The King of Hearts called for the tarts
And beat the Knave full sore.
The Knave of Hearts brought back the tarts
And vowed he'd steal no more.

Jack Be Nimble

Jack be nimble,
Jack be quick,
Jack jump over
The candlestick.

Index